The
FORBIDDEN
FARM

THE COBWEB KIDS #2

JOHN C. ABRAHAMSON

TO MY COBWEB KIDS

Olivia, Jack and Caleb

CONTENTS

SUMMER BREAK

The Carolina blue sky was as calm as can be. The air was thick and heavy, as it usually is during the month of August, but the Bailey kids didn't mind.

Olivia, Jack and Caleb were all in their bathing suits, running through the sprinkler in their driveway, trying to keep cool.

The kids were on Summer Break, and

enjoying the last couple of days before they had to go back to school.

Olivia, the oldest child, with beautiful red hair and freckles, was heading into the third grade.

Jack, the middle child, with blonde hair and blue eyes, was seven years old, but was turning eight years old in November when he'll be in second grade.

Then there was the youngest brother Caleb, or Wub for short, and had dark hair. He was heading into Kindergarten.

Mrs. Bailey was outside watching the kids play as she worked in the family garden.

Mr. Bailey was inside the house, getting ready to head to a local farm for a project he was working on for Halloween.

The Bailey family was really into

Halloween. They enjoyed shopping for costumes, they liked trick or treating, and they loved jumping out from behind closed doors to scare each other.

Especially the boys.

Mr. Bailey had a meeting at a local farm, to discuss a haunted attraction idea that he had.

Mr. Bailey wanted to start his own corn maze, haunted trail and 3D maze during the month of October.

Earlier in the year, Olivia had her first haunted house experience, when she and the entire Bailey family went on a long road trip for Spring Break.

Olivia and her Dad went into The Haunted Mansion, and they had a blast.

They had so much fun!

Mr. Bailey was starting his own haunted attraction, but the only difference between the haunted house he and Olivia went into, and the attraction he was starting, was that this attraction would be outside.

It was on a farm, and not in a mansion. So his entire haunted attraction would be outside, and not in a house.

Mr. Bailey grabbed the keys to his car and headed downstairs.

"Kids, Dad is heading to the farm for a few hours. I'll be back in time for dinner."

They didn't hear him. Or maybe they did, but they weren't listening.

The kids were having too much fun playing in the water.

Mr. Bailey opened the trunk of his car in the garage and placed some large posters in the back.

Jack noticed.

"Dad, wait!" he said. "Where are you going?"

Dad smiled.

"I'm heading to the farm to walk through the trail, so we can plan the haunted farm for Halloween."

Jack ran up to his Dad.

"Cool!" he exclaimed. "Can I go with you?"

"Sure, Bud," Dad responded. "Go inside and dry off quickly, because we have to leave very soon."

"Okay, I'll be right back."

Jack grabbed a beach towel and dried off in the garage, before he went into the house to change his clothes.

Mrs. Bailey said to Jack before he went inside the house, "Make sure you dry your feet off too, so you don't slip going up the stairs!"

"Okay!" Jack yelled excitedly.

Olivia and Caleb continued to play in the water while Dad opened the car door and waited for Jack inside of the car.

A few minutes later, Jack came running back downstairs wearing his gym shorts and a t-shirt and jumped into the backseat of the car.

Mr. Bailey and Jack waved to Olivia, Caleb and Mom as they backed the car out of the garage, and drove away.

They had a little bit of a drive towards Lake Norman to get to the farm, so Jack and Dad talked a little bit about their day ahead.

Normally, Mr. Bailey would blast really loud music when he and Jack would go out for a drive together.

But not today.

Jack asked his Dad all kinds of questions.

"Will we see any creepy Halloween stuff today?" Jack asked.

"I don't think so Bud," Dad replied. "Today is just a walk-through."

"What's a walk-through?" Jack inquired.

"That means we are just going to walk around the entire farm, to start planning what the trail will look like."

"You mean it's not even built yet?"

"That's right. There is still a lot of work for us to do to get ready for October, when the Haunted Farm opens," Dad explained. "This is really just the beginning."

"Cool," Jack said eagerly. "It will be fun to watch you build it from start to finish!"

"Indeed. We'll have to take lots of

pictures, so when the farm is ready to open for Halloween, we can look back to see how much progress we made."

Mr. Bailey turned off of the main road into the farm, and drove down this long dirt road towards the parking lot.

Dad parked the car, and he and Jack got out and walked towards the pond where the farmers were waiting for them.

For the next couple of hours, Mr. Bailey, his son Jack, and the farmer with his wife walked through the entire woods and trails of their farm.

They talked and talked about where the trail would go, and also had planned the direction and length of the haunted trail.

They also decided that they would have a 3D maze, after people walked through the haunted wooded trail. Guests would even have to wear 3D glasses.

And then after the 3D maze, there would be a corn maze where people in Halloween costumes would be waiting to jump out and scare them.

They were all excited and ready to begin building the trail.

After they were done walking the trail, Jack and Dad got back into the car and started to drive home.

Jack was tired after all of the hiking, and it was hot outside under the blazing Summer sun.

"So now what?" Jack asked his Dad.

"Now, we go home, and Dad has to begin mapping out the trail."

"Didn't we just do that?" Jack asked.

"We came up with a plan today, but Dad is going to actually draw it on a large poster board, and begin planning where all the scary parts will be," Dad explained. "Now the real work begins."

MAPPED OUT

Mr. Bailey and Jack had arrived back at home later that afternoon. Jack ran upstairs to tell Olivia and Caleb about his trip to the farm.

Mr. Bailey drank a glass of water and then placed his laptop on the kitchen table.

He pressed the power button and sat down in the chair while he watched the laptop boot up.

Jack came back downstairs to see what his Dad was up to next.

"What's up, Bud?" Dad said.

Jack inched closer to see what was on the computer.

"I wanted to see what you were going to do next," Jack said.

"Well, first I'm going to use Google Maps on the internet to get satellite pictures of the farm," Dad explained.

"What do you mean?" Jack asked.

"To start planning the haunted trail, we need to make a map. So, I'm going to print out pictures of the farm, and tape it to a poster board."

"So you can draw the map on the poster board?"

"Exactly!" Dad said. "Today, when we walked around the farm, we had some ideas of what the trails and paths would look like. Now I'm just going to draw it out."

"Cool!" Jack said.

"Once this map is complete, we can hand out copies to the carpenters at the farm, so they can start building all of the stations on the trail."

"What do you mean by *stations*?" Jack asked.

"After we know which direction everyone will be walking on the trail, we need to plan what scary places will be on the trail. Those places are called stations."

Jack thought about it for a minute.

Jack questioned, "Do you mean you have to plan where on the trail people in costumes will jump out at people to scare them?"

"Yes! That's exactly what I mean."

"That sounds fun," Jack said.

"It *is* fun!" Dad replied. "Planning out all of the scares on the trail is one of the best parts."

"Do you have any planned yet?" Jack was curious.

"Of course," Dad responded. "For starters, after people pay for their ticket to enter, I want to build a large temple maze."

"Temple maze? Awesome!"

"Thanks. I thought that sounded pretty cool too. We'll build a tall dark pyramid for people to walk into, and then inside the temple, will be a completely dark maze. Everyone will have to find their way through the maze without being able to see anything."

"Will this be at night time?" Jack asked.

"Yes, it will. The haunted farm won't open until the sun goes down. That just helps make it scarier for everyone that attends."

"I agree. That sounds creepy," Jack said. "Will there be anyone inside the dark maze in a scary costume?"

"I don't want to give all of my secrets away, but I plan on having people *above* the maze."

"Above the maze? How will you do that?" Jack wondered.

"We'll place thick pieces of wood on top of the maze, like a ceiling. Then people in costumes will be able to stand on the ceiling, so when customers walk by, they can reach down through several openings and scare them."

"Whoa!" Jack was fascinated. "What happens when they get out of the temple maze?"

"I can't tell you everything, but how about when it's done being built, I'll take you there to show you?"

"Really?" Jack said.

"Really!" Dad responded.

"Awesome! At night time?" Jack asked.

"We'll see…" Dad said. "Maybe to start, I'll take you by the farm when they're still building it in the daylight."

Dad paused.

"I don't want to take you at night when we're open, in case you get too scared."

"I won't get too scared, I know it's all pretend."

"Yes, but Mom may not like you going at night. We will see as time gets closer."

"Okay," Jack said. "I'm going to head upstairs and tell Olivia and Caleb."

Jack ran upstairs excited to tell his brother and sister.

Mr. Bailey continued to work on drawing his map on the poster board; which included numbers of where every scare on the trail would be.

When Jack got upstairs, Olivia and Caleb were both playing a board game.

"What are you both playing?" Jack said.

"Caleb and I are playing a math game for SPARK," Olivia said.

"Yeah, and Olivia is cheating," Caleb

said.

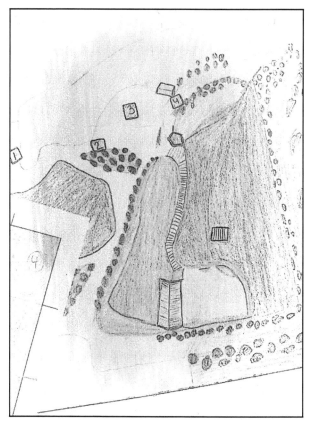

"I am not," Olivia snapped back at her youngest brother.

Wub was very competitive and really did not like to lose, at anything.

SPARK was a program that their school sponsored every Summer.

The students at the school would pledge a certain amount of hours towards SPARK before Summer Break.

Most students said that they would achieve at least one hundred hours of SPARK during the Summer.

That meant they would spend at least one hundred hours doing something that had to do with reading or math.

It could be anything.

Reading or math board games, going to museums, reading books, or even playing educational video games.

Anything.

The goal was to have all of the students from school learning during the Summer, so when they got back to school in the Fall, they not only don't forget how to read or do math, but to actually improve their skills.

Caleb and Olivia were playing an educational board game, so it was counting towards their SPARK hours.

If students hit their goal by the end of Summer, they would win prizes when they got back to school.

Prizes such as free ice cream, and other special items depending on how many hours they had completed.

Some students even completed over three hundred hours of reading and math during the Summer Break.

That was really amazing.

That meant those kids spent several hours every day doing some kind of math or reading during the Summer.

The Bailey kids probably completed several hundred hours too, since they traveled to lots of museums and educational places regularly.

They just didn't always track all of their hours.

"Want to know what Dad just told me?" Jack asked them excitedly.

"No!" they both responded.

"We're trying to play a game," Wub barked back in a crabby voice.

"You're just mad because Olivia is probably beating you again at that game."

That just made Wub even more upset.

"I am not losing, she cheated," Caleb roared as he left the room.

"Jack!" Dad yelled from downstairs.

"Stop picking on your brother."

Jack and Olivia snickered.

Mrs. Bailey checked on Caleb to make sure he was okay, as Jack went back downstairs to see what his Dad was up to now.

Mr. Bailey had the car keys in his hand.

"Where are you going now, Dad?" Jack said.

"I'm off to Morris Costumes," Dad said.

"What are you going to get there?" Jack enquired.

"I have to go pick up the paint for the 3D maze. Want to come with me?"

"Do I?" Jack's eyes got wide. "Of course I want to go!"

"Okay then. Let's go. They close in

thirty minutes, and they're waiting for me."

THE COSTUME STORE

Mr. Bailey and Jack pulled up to the loading dock behind the Morris Costumes warehouse.

There were several men waiting for them with gallons of paint in their hands.

"I thought we were going to a costume store?" Jack said.

"Well, sort of." Dad said. "This is the

warehouse where they keep all of the supplies that they sell wholesale."

"What does wholesale mean?" Jack said.

"It means they are selling us lots of paint for a lower price than what customers would pay normally."

"Why would they have you pay less money for paint than other people?" Jack said.

"Because we will be buying lots of paint every year for this Halloween business." Dad tried to explain.

Mr. Bailey pressed a button from the front seat of his car, and the trunk door automatically opened up.

Mr. Bailey got out of the car and greeted the men on the loading dock.

After loading all of the paint buckets into

the trunk, Mr. Bailey closed the trunk, and then opened Jack's backseat door.

"Want to go inside of the warehouse?" Dad asked. "They thought you'd like to get a quick tour of the cool Halloween props that they have."

"Awesome!" Jack exclaimed.

"They close in a few minutes but they said we can do a quick walkthrough," Dad said.

Jack hopped out of the car and he and his Dad followed the men inside.

Inside of the warehouse were large rooms full of big Halloween props, like inflatable monsters that people put on the front of their lawn during the month of October.

Other rooms had boxes and boxes filled

with costumes.

"These containers of costumes will soon be shipped to all of the party and Halloween stores around the state," one of the men explained.

They kept walking to view some of the other rooms in the warehouse.

"Do you know what you want to be for Halloween yet?" he asked Jack.

Jack gave it some thought.

"I want to be a cowboy or a sheriff," Jack responded.

The man smiled, "Oh yes, that's a popular one for boys your age."

The man reached into one of the boxes and tossed Jack a package.

It was a sheriff costume!

"Is that the kind of costume you're

looking for?" he asked Jack.

"Yes, this is awesome!" Jack said excitedly.

"Well its yours if Dad says it's okay."

Mr. Bailey smiled and nodded.

"What do you say, Bud?" Dad said.

Jacks eyes lit up. "Thanks!"

"You're very welcome," the man replied. "Now the other boxes you need are in this room."

They walked through another door, to a room with more stacked boxes and other gallons of paint.

"These two boxes here have all the items from the list you sent us."

Mr. Bailey peaked into one of the boxes and saw a pile of scary masks and costumes.

"Perfect. Thank you," Dad said.

"We'll help you carry them out to your car."

The two other men that helped load the paint into the car earlier, came back to carry the costume boxes to the car.

After the boxes were loaded into the back of the car, Mr. Bailey shook hands with the Morris Costumes employees, and he and Jack got back into the car.

"Now what?" Jack asked.

"Now we head to the farm to drop off the materials so they can move forward with construction and orientation," Dad said.

"What do you mean?" Jack said.

"The carpenters building all of the sets on the trail need this paint for construction; and the costumes will be needed for all of the people that will wear the costumes on the trail."

"I get that," Jack said. "But what is orientation?"

"Ah, I see," Dad said. "Orientation is when all of the people that will be working at the haunted farm, learn about their job. They find out which costume they get to wear. They find out their schedule. Then they have to sign paperwork so they can get paid."

"Sounds a lot like when I start school," Jack said. "When I meet my teachers and get my assigned desk."

"That's pretty accurate, Bud. It's very much like that." Dad said.

"Only I don't get paid."

Dad laughed out loud.

A little while later, Jack and Mr. Bailey arrived back at the farm. Dad dropped all of the paint off in the barn.

Dad then loaded the two boxes full of costumes and props into the shed down by the trail entrance.

Mr. Bailey grabbed a spray can of bright orange paint out of the shed.

"Come on, Bud," he said.

"What are we doing?" Jack said.

"We're going to mark the trail," Dad said.

"Mark the trail? For what?" Jack said.

"We're going to paint big orange arrows on the ground along the trail so the builders know which way the haunted trail will go. That way they can start clearing the trail of debris, and start building the sets that I had drawn back at the house on my poster map."

Dad started marking the trail like he said, and not more than ten minutes later, a big tractor came from around the corner, and began following his arrows to mow the trail.

CONSTRUCTION

Two weeks had passed before Jack and his Dad had visited the farm.

During those two weeks, Mr. Bailey finished drawing all of the stations and gave them to the workers at the farm that were building the scares on the trail.

Olivia, Jack and Caleb were all back at school.

It was less than one month before the haunted trail would be open to the public.

Forbidden Farms was the name they chose to call it.

Since it had been a few weeks when they last visited the farm, Mr. Bailey thought it made sense to stop by and check in on the progress of the construction.

He wanted to make sure that everything was being built properly and on time.

As usual, Jack was curious and wanted to join his Dad. Jack thought it was fun to watch the haunted attraction get built from the very beginning.

Caleb and Olivia also wanted to go with them this time.

After school, Mr. Bailey and his three children drove down the dirt road to an open field.

That was the farm parking lot. It was right next to the cornfield that was being cut down to make the maze.

The kids were immediately excited as soon as they hopped out of the back seat of the car. They saw the entrance of the trail being built.

A large haunted temple!

The shape of the temple was a Mayan pyramid, and only half of it was painted.

There were several farm employees painting black lines on the front of the temple, to make it look like large bricks.

The kids ran over to the front of the temple. It was huge!

"Dad, how tall is this temple?" Jack asked.

"It's about twenty feet tall," Dad replied.

"That's like five of me," Caleb said.

They all laughed.

"Do you kids want to walk the entire trail with me now?" Dad asked.

They all screamed, "YEEEESSSSSS!"

Mr. Bailey already knew that answer.

"Okay, let's start by walking through the front door of the temple," Dad said.

Jack ran in front of Olivia and Caleb to be the first one through the door.

"Careful Jack, they're still building this, so it may not be completely safe yet," Dad said.

"Okay, I'll be careful," Jack responded.

"And no running," Olivia added.

Jack and Caleb rolled their eyes; they both knew she was imitating their Dad.

When they walked through the front door opening of the temple, they had found themselves in a narrow hallway.

"Is this a maze?" Olivia asked.

"Sort of," Dad said. "When it's dark outside in the evening, you won't be able to see anything when you walk through the temple."

"It will be dark?" Caleb asked.

"Completely dark," Dad said. "It's not really a maze, but when everyone has to feel around for the walls to get through it, they will think it's a maze."

The Bailey kids continued walking through the temple maze.

"When the maze is finished being built, there will be a roof on it too," Dad continued.

"In case it rains?" Olivia asked.

Dad smiled. "Actually, it's so one of the workers in a costume can walk above the guests and scare them from up above."

The kids thought that was crazy.

"So when people walk through the dark maze at night, they also have to worry about someone grabbing them from the ceiling?" Olivia asked.

"Nobody is going to grab the customers, but they will definitely be scared!" Dad said.

They finished walking through the temple, and came to a somewhat steep hill. There was a pile of wood at the top of the hill.

"What's going here?" Jack asked.

"A slide," Dad responded.

"A slide? Really?" Jack said.

"Yup!" Dad said. "The hill is too steep for people to walk down in the dark."

"Especially when people are trying to scare them," Olivia said.

"That's right," Dad said. "Not to mention, the ground may be wet and slippery. And there will be fallen leaves on the ground. We can't have anyone get hurt. Being safe is our number one goal."

"Will anyone ever get hurt?" Olivia asked.

"It will happen," Dad said. "Probably nothing ever serious. Maybe someone will trip, fall and scrape their knee. That's really hard to stop. That can happen anywhere."

"Especially at night time in the dark," Jack said.

"Exactly right," Dad responded.

Mr. Bailey and his three children walked carefully down the steep hill into the woods.

They continued walking along the trail through the woods, where they hiked by many areas that were still under construction.

It was hard to tell what they were building, unless they looked at the drawings that Mr. Bailey drew.

Many of the scares had piles of wood, or other raw materials.

But there were many farm employees walking around that were working on getting the sets assembled.

The kids saw someone walk by them in the distance, with a shovel.

"Dad, look!" Olivia exclaimed.

"What is he going to be digging?" Jack asked.

"Hard to tell," Dad said. "He could be digging a hole to cement a wooden post into the ground."

"Like the temple?" Wub asked.

"Yes, like the temple," Dad replied. "But I think he may be digging a hole for the graveyard."

"How can you tell?" Olivia asked.

Dad pointed towards a large garbage barrel near where the man was about to dig.

"Well," Dad said. "See that barrel over there? He's going to bury that into the ground."

"Why?" Wub asked.

"So we can have someone hide in the ground behind a tombstone," Dad replied.

"Cool!!!!!!" Jack said. "It will look like a monster is coming out of the cemetery."

"That sounds scary," Olivia said.

Mr. Bailey smiled.

"That's the point, Beauty," Dad said. "Some people will scream and run away, and others will laugh. That's part of the fun."

They continued walking through the woods.

There was already an existing trail that from the previous tractor rides at the farm. The farmers offered rides to customers that picked pumpkins at their farm.

They could see that the workers have been busy clearing a wider path in the woods, to make it safer for people to walk at night.

They cut down branches that were sticking out, and cut down anything in the ground that was sticking up before, such as roots from older trees or shrubs.

They also saw that there was an electrician placing plug outlets around the farm. That way they can have some lights for people to see where they were walking in the dark.

The kids remembered that their Dad recently said "Safety first!"

The Bailey family continued walking through the woods, and crossed over what looked like a brand new bridge.

The farmers had a mini-bridge built so their customers could cross a small little creek that passed through the forest.

After crossing the bridge, they walked up a small hill to a place where the landscape had changed.

The trees were skinnier and looked more organized, almost like they were planted in rows a long time ago.

If that wasn't different enough, the kids also noticed that the entire wooded area at the top of the hill, was wrapped in yarn.

A few feet off of the ground, yarn was tied to all of the trees.

"What's with all of the string?" Jack asked.

"This is where we are putting the 3D maze," Dad said.

"3D maze?" Wub asked.

"Yup. Every customer will be given a pair of cardboard 3D glasses, before they walk through the maze."

"How will the 3D glasses help when walking through the yarn maze?" Olivia was curious.

Dad laughed.

"Great question, Beauty." Dad replied. "The maze isn't done yet. I recently walked through here and made a maze out of the yarn. But the employees that were working on all of the construction will replace the yarn with eight foot tall walls."

"Whoa. What will the walls be made out of?" Jack asked.

"We're using rolls of black landscaping tarp. Kind of like the large rolls of foil or plastic wrap that we use for your school lunches," Dad said. "But *much* larger."

"What happens when everyone walks through a maze of eight foot black walls?" Olivia asked.

"The first step is putting up the black

canvas," Dad said. "But the next step is painting the walls full of pictures, so when people walk through with their 3D glasses, the pictures look like they're coming out of the walls right at you."

"Just like when we go to watch 3D movies," Wub said.

"Precisely," Dad said with a grin.

Wub always had extra little comments to say; that's why they sometimes called him Two Cents.

They continued walking.

After following the path out of the forest, they came upon a cornfield.

The future corn maze.

The kids noticed something odd. Most of the corn was several feet taller than the rest of the corn.

"Hey Dad?" they all seemed to ask at once.

"I know what you're going to ask," Dad said. "Why is some of the corn much shorter than the rest?"

The kids nodded.

"The short answer is that corn is like grass. It grows back after you cut it. I learned that the hard way," Dad sighed.

"The hard way?" Jack asked.

"Yeah... This is the corn maze. A few weeks ago, I actually used a lawn mower to cut the layout of the maze. Then when I returned from a business trip, I saw that what I cut had already grown back. That's why some of the corn is a few feet shorter than the rest of the cornfield. It grew back after I cut it."

The kids found that fascinating.

"Do you have to cut it again?" Olivia asked.

"Well, now that the obvious path of the maze is cut, the farmers will have people re-cut the maze," Dad said.

"At least you don't have to cut it again," Wub said.

"If you are open the entire month of October, will the farmers have to keep cutting the corn to keep it short?" Jack asked.

"Great question," Dad said. "And the answer is NO. We won't have to keep cutting the corn during the month of October. Want to guess why?"

The kids looked deep in thought.

"Because it won't rain that much?"

Olivia said.

"Great guess, Beauty. Usually October in North Carolina is a fairly dry month," Dad said. "But the actual reason is because the more customers that walk through the maze, the more worn the path will be."

"Like how our soccer field at school doesn't have much grass, because we always play on it?" Jack said.

"You kids are so smart," Dad said smiling.

The Bailey family walked out of the corn maze and found themselves in the parking lot where they started.

They walked one large loop around the farm.

"That's it kids. Thanks for walking through with me," Dad said.

"Will we be able to walk through it again after you open for Halloween?" Jack asked.

Dad knew that question was coming.

"I'll think about it. I can certainly have you all walk through the trail with me again in the daylight, but I don't know about at night time when we are open. I don't want to scare you."

"Or have rotten nightmares," Wub said, adding his two cents.

"That's right Wub. I don't want you to have nightmares," Dad said.

OPENING NIGHT

It was opening night!

After months of hard work and preparation, Forbidden Farm was finally open to the public.

But there was still a lot of work that had to be done, so Mr. Bailey was heading to the farm early that day.

Of course, a certain someone wanted to

join him.

Mr. Bailey looked at Jack.

"Can I help you?" Dad asked.

Jack grinned.

"You know what," Jack said.

"You want to come with me," Dad said.

"Of course I want to go with you," Jack said.

Dad replied. "We have the entire month of October for you to come with me, Bud."

Jack frowned.

Mr. Bailey knew that Jack really wanted to go with him. Jack just stared at his Dad with disappointment.

"Okay. You can come with me, but you need to behave and do exactly as I say. I'm going to be very busy and won't have time to play around," Dad said.

"Yesssssssssss!!!!!" Jack shouted.

"I mean it," Dad said. "We can't do five potty breaks, and I can't feed you every twenty minutes. I have to work all around the farm tonight."

"I promise. I'll be good," Jack replied.

"Okay, grab your sweatshirt. It's going to get chilly when the sun goes down," Dad said.

Jack opened his closet and saw his sweatshirt on a hangar. He grabbed the sweatshirt, but he didn't put it on.

Instead, Jack put on his sheriff costume that he got from Morris Costumes.

Dad smiled as Jack came running downstairs to put his shoes on.

"Cool costume, Bud."

They arrived at the farm a little while

later and the parking lot was fairly empty.

"Where is everybody?" Jack asked.

"It's still early. Guests won't start showing up for a few more hours when it gets dark outside," Dad said.

"Why are we here so early?"

"Because of orientation."

"Oh yeah, I remember you telling me about orientation," Jack said.

"That's right. Everyone shows up today to fill out their paperwork, and finish training."

"I remember you said they fill out forms so they can get paid," Jack said.

"They also complete emergency contact forms, in case they get hurt and we need to call someone."

"Wouldn't you call 9-1-1 if they get

hurt?" Jack said.

"That's right. We would call 9-1-1 if someone got hurt really bad. But that won't happen. So we ask for someone that they know who we can call. Like a Mom or Dad, so we can let them know."

"What kind of injury could someone get?" Jack asked.

"Some employees can step on a branch or something, and roll their ankle. If something like that happens, we'd call their emergency contact, not 9-1-1."

Mr. Bailey and Jack walked down to the crowd of people near the rock quarry.

Jack saw that many people were sitting at picnic tables, filling out their paperwork. He also saw some people trying on their costumes.

"Hey Bud," Dad said. "Why don't you go over there and roast yourself some hotdogs while I check in on a few things."

"Cool!" Jack said.

"Just ask my friend over there by the grill to help you, and he'll make sure you get everything that you need.

Mr. Bailey walked away as Jack made his way towards one of the several fire pits. Jack asked his Dad's friend for a roasting stick and a hotdog.

The man stuck two hotdogs onto the end of a pointed stick and handed it to Jack.

He also made sure that Jack kept a safe distance away from the logs in the fire. Jack started roasting his hotdogs.

A few minutes later, Dad came back with a walkie-talkie radio. He turned it on and off to make sure that it worked and didn't need new batteries.

Jack sat on a tree stump, eating his hotdogs. He watched a bunch of the employees walk into the woods with their costumes on.

"Are they getting ready?" Jack said.

"Yeah. We still don't open for another hour, but we don't want all forty employees sitting down here in their costumes when the guests arrive," Dad said.

"What's the radio for?" Jack said. "Is it yours?"

"It's mine while I'm here, but not mine to keep. My job every night at the farm is to walk around behind the scenes to make sure everything is running smoothly. And if anyone needs help with something, we use our radios to communicate."

"What kind of help would they need?" Jack said.

"Could be anything, really. Maybe they need a bathroom break. So I'll fill in while they step away. Or maybe they need some extra materials. Like more bottles of liquid for the fog machines."

"Fog machines?" Jack was fascinated.

"Yes, we have several fog machines out there in the woods," Dad smiled.

"What do we do for the next hour?" Jack questioned.

"I have to go light the Tiki torches at the entrance. Want to go for a walk?" Dad asked.

Jack nodded.

"Take the last couple of bites of your

hotdogs and lets go."

Jack finished his last two bites and then wiped the ketchup and mustard off of his hands with a napkin.

He threw his paper plate and soiled napkin into the trash barrel and walked towards the entrance of the farm with his Dad.

Mr. Bailey took out a book of matches from his pocket and had lit the two wicks of the Tiki torches at the entrance to the farm.

It was getting darker, so the flames on top of the torches made the Forbidden Farm sign look really spooky.

Several cars turned off of the main road and onto the dirt road entrance of the farm towards the parking lot.

They drove past Jack and his Dad as they walked back towards the quarry.

Many cars started to park in the parking lot.

"Looks like people are beginning to show up!" Jack said excitedly.

"Sure looks like it," Dad said. "I don't expect a huge crowd tonight. It should get busier as Halloween gets closer."

Mr. Bailey and Jack walked towards the ticket booth.

"Are we ready to go?" Mr. Bailey asked the woman in the ticket booth.

"Yessir, we're ready to open!" she replied.

"Okay, I'm going to walk the trail and perform one last check before we send the first group through. I want to wait until its completely dark outside anyways, so we still have about twenty more minutes."

The women behind the ticket counter leaned over and smiled at Jack in his sheriff costume.

"Looks like you and your Dad will be our first customers!" she said.

Jack was getting excited. He couldn't wait to walk the trail in the dark with his Dad.

Mr. Bailey raised the walkie-talkie to his mouth, pressed the button and spoke into it after he heard a beeping sound.

"Okay team, I'm going to walk through the trail right now to check on y'all before we open. If you have any questions, now will be the time to ask," Mr. Bailey said.

Jack walked passed a scarecrow as they

headed towards the front of the temple maze entrance.

"Hey, I don't remember this being here," Jack said.

The scarecrow moved towards Jack.

Jack shouted in fear.

Mr. Bailey laughed.

"I hope that's a sign of things to come for all of our customers this month. She startled you good!" Dad said.

THE TEMPLE

Jack and Mr. Bailey made their way to the front entrance of the temple maze. This was the first time that Jack had seen it completed.

Last time they visited, it was still being built and only half of it was painted.

Jack thought it looked awesome now that the bricks were painted, and real vines were hanging over it just like they do in a jungle.

Mr. Bailey took out the matches to light up the Tiki torches, just as he did for the torches at the entrance to the farm.

The line of customers started to build and get longer.

Jack could feel the excitement of opening night all around him. The employees seemed animated, the customers in line were excited, and Jack could see that his Dad was quite anxious too.

"Okay team, I'm about to do a test walkthrough with my son Jack," Mr. Bailey said into the radio, as he turned to look at Jack. "Ready?" he asked.

"Yes! Let's go!" Jack shouted.

Mr. Bailey talked into the radio again.

"Can we get the music soundtrack turned on please?"

A few seconds later, Jack looked up into the trees, and noticed that spooky Halloween sounds began coming out of the music speakers that were mounted in the treetops.

"Okay, let's go," Dad said.

They both walked into the maze.

It was completely dark.

Jack reached his hands out to feel the walls around him, since he couldn't see anything in front of him.

Jack heard loud sounds of werewolves, ghosts howling and heavy metal chains clanging.

The music soundtrack also had eerie music playing with the sound effects.

Mr. Bailey walked ahead, since he had the path of the maze memorized. He waited for Jack at the exit.

Jack jumped from a loud sound, as someone banged a shovel against the maze wall from the outside.

As Jack finally made it to the exit of the maze, and saw his Dad, he knew something else was going to jump out at him, because Mr. Bailey was smirking.

Just then, Jack saw an arm reach down from the ceiling above the maze to grab Jack. The arm looked like a skeleton costume.

Jack was so focused on the darkness of the maze, he forgot that his Dad previously told him about the rooftop monster.

"So what do you think so far?" Mr.

Bailey asked Jack.

"You were right," Jack said. "It's quite different walking through it in the dark."

"We have more people in the maze that will jump out at customers. I just walked ahead of you to tell them all to take it easy on you, since this is your first time in a haunted maze."

"I like the music and creepy sounds coming from the speakers in the woods," Jack added.

"We added the speakers this week. We had an electrician run a wire through the top of the trees around the entire farm," Dad said.

"So there is music playing everywhere on the trail?" Jack asked.

"Well, not everywhere. We don't have music in the corn maze. The wires aren't just for the music speakers either, it's also to provide power for the lights, fog machines and other things that need electricity," Dad explained.

"Wow, is this the slide?" Jack said.

Jack was referring to the big dome shaped tunnel right after the temple maze.

Last time Jack visited, it was still under construction.

"That's right. Want to slide down it first?" Dad asked.

"Sure. The slide is huge!" Jack said.

"It had to be. We can't let guests walking down this steep hill in the dark, especially if the leaves are wet."

"I like that the slide is covered with a black tarp too," Jack added.

Mr. Bailey motioned for Jack to climb into the slide to go to the bottom.

Jack climbed up onto the ledge of the

slide, and all he saw was darkness. He turned to look at this Dad, then down he went.

Mr. Bailey heard Jack belt out a loud *Yahooooooo* that echoed for ten seconds.

Mr. Bailey went down the slide next, and saw Jack at the bottom.

"That was fun!" Jack said. "I was waiting for someone to jump out and scare me."

"That's a great idea to place someone in the slide, or at the bottom; but this is really just to get people safely down the hill. Maybe we can change that though as Halloween gets closer and the crowds get larger. The more scares the better."

They turned their attention to the next stop on the trail, which was dimly lit.

The next station on the trail, looked far away, but it was only about fifty feet. It looked like it was further away because the only thing they could see was one little spotlight.

"What's that light up ahead?" Jack said.

"We'll have to keep walking and find out," Dad said with a grin.

"It looks like some kind of railroad track," Jack replied.

"Let's keep going Bud. It gets better," Dad said.

THE TRAIL

Jack was right, it was a railroad track that he saw in the distance. But it was a short track that was on a steep hill facing in their direction.

Jack and Mr. Bailey stopped at the bottom of the hill, where the railroad track ended by their feet.

They stood there in silence.

They could hear the faint music and sound effects in the distance, but it wasn't as loud as it was when they walked through the temple maze.

After a few seconds, they saw movement at the top of the hill where the railroad track began.

It was a mining train cart, and it was speeding down the train track right at them.

Jack's eyes opened really wide in fear as he thought the mining cart was going to run him over.

Jack was ready to dive out of the way, but his Dad put his hands on his shoulders, as if he should stand still to wait and see what happened.

Just before the mining train got to them, it stopped immediately at the bottom of the track.

The mining cart tilted forward and a large human figure popped out and flew over their head.

Jack crouched to the ground and covered his head with his arms thinking the figure would land on him.

But it didn't.

He noticed after it flew over him, that it was a pretend monster, and it was attached to a wire.

It coasted right over him.

"Wow," Jack said. "That was crazy. I thought the mining cart was going to hit us."

"That's how we built it. It worked exactly how I hoped it would," Dad said.

"And what was that thing that came out

of the train?" Jack asked.

"That was a mannequin with a costume on," Dad replied. "We hooked it up to a wire so when it launches out of the mining cart it floats above everyone without landing on them."

Jack turned to see someone else in a costume come from behind them.

The person had the mannequin in his hands and walked it back to the top of the hill.

Mr. Bailey held Jack's hand as they continued walking through the trail onto the next station.

"What was that guy doing?" Jack said.

"He was resetting the mining cart," Dad replied. "To get it ready for the next group of people that walk through. When we open in a few minutes, we'll be sending groups of people through every couple of minutes."

"So he has to reset the mining train cart for every group that walks through?" Jack asked.

"That's right. Same for everybody else that works here. They have to reset their station for every single group. It's actually a lot of work."

"They must get tired," Jack said.

"They should be okay tonight, but as Halloween gets closer, we will get busier and busier every weekend."

"How many groups will come through on a weekend?" Jack asked.

"At least two hundred groups," Dad replied. "On a busy Friday or Saturday evening, we can have over one thousand people come through in an evening."

"Wow!" Jack said. "That's like two hundred times he'd have to reset the mining cart."

"That's right. It's a lot of work," Dad said. "They enjoy it though. Where else can you get paid to scare thousands of people for fun?"

"It must hurt their voice too," Jack added.

"It actually does," Dad said. "When you yell and shout all night many people do lose their voice."

They kept walking onto the next section of the wooded trail. Jack saw a wooden sign up ahead that read The Cemetery.

Jack stopped and stared at his Dad.

"Is this a real graveyard?" Jack said.

"It is for the next month," Dad said.

"I'm serious."

Mr. Bailey could see that Jack was a bit tense.

"It's not a real graveyard, but we do have plenty of zombies that will pop-out in there."

They walked into the cemetery where Jack saw a bunch of tombstones. He could tell that they weren't made of stone like real ones that he'd see in actual graveyards.

"Styrofoam," Dad said. "They're sheets of Styrofoam that we cut and painted gray to make them look like stone. Kind of like the temple."

Jack noticed something else as they walked through the cemetery.

Fog.

Jack remembered that his Dad said there were fog machines throughout the farm to make it look spookier.

Just then, the ground moved near Jack's feet and he saw a monster come out of the ground! Jack screamed louder than ever.

After a moment, Jack remembered that it was an actor, and it was all pretend.

He had nothing to worry about.

"That was the scariest one so far," Jack said.

"That's one of my favorites actually," Dad said. "Remember I said we buried garbage cans into the ground for our actors to hide in them? It looks like they crawl out of the dirt, when they really don't."

Jack chuckled. That was kind of silly to think about them just sitting for hours in garbage cans all night.

They made their way through the rest of the cemetery as Mr. Bailey quickly stopped and talked to the rest of the actors, to make sure that they had everything they needed.

They were about to open in a few minutes, and let the first group through the temple maze.

The next section of the woods had a big sign over the trail, that read Phobia Forest.

"Phobia Forest?" Jack said. "What does that mean?"

"A phobia is when you are afraid of something. Like being scared of heights, or scared of the dark. Those are phobias," Dad explained.

"I don't like spiders," Jack said.

"Being scared of spiders is called Arachnophobia," Dad replied.

"What phobia stations do you have in this part of the trail?" Jack questioned.

"You'll find out in a minute. We have a couple of different ones. Let's move through it quickly though, since I need to give the okay to start letting guests through," Dad said.

Jack knew immediately what the first phobia scare was. He walked straight ahead, and the trail got narrower and narrower.

Eventually, he came to an entrance, which looked like a tunnel in the middle of the woods.

Not just any tunnel though.

An incredibly narrow tunnel.

So narrow that you'd have to turn sideways to get through it.

"This one is call claustrophobia," Dad

said. "It means being scared of tight spaces."

Jack just stood there.

"We can walk around this one," Dad said.

They continued on, passing several phobias on the way. Again, Mr. Bailey kept checking with the workers to make sure everyone was ready to start the evening.

Jack looked up, and saw something that he wish he hadn't.

A giant seven foot spider.

Not just any spider. A black widow. He could tell by the bright red hourglass shape that was on its body.

The light was shining right on it.

What made it worse, was that it came down from its massive web and landed right on Jack.

Mr. Bailey grabbed the giant fake spider and tugged the rope it was attached to. "Cool," Dad said. "Glad this one works."

One of the employees behind the tree pulled the rope and the spider went back up into the tree where it started, ready for the next guest to walk buy.

The other trees had figures tied to them, wrapped in large spider webs. They used the bags of cobwebs that you can buy at the store during Halloween.

The kind you see on people's front porch when you go trick or treating.

"Of course you had a giant spider land on me," Jack said. "Did you know I was scared of spiders?"

"Most people are," Dad replied.

THE 3D MAZE

Jack and his Dad had crossed back across the wooded trail and entered another section of the farm.

This section had a completely different landscape than Phobia Forest and the Cemetery.

This area had more rolling hills and tall skinny pine trees.

Jack knew where they were headed.

The 3D maze.

Jack also remembered that they had to walk down one hill before walking up another hill to get there.

Jack looked up and saw a large billboard sign with an arrow pointing the way for them to go.

"Do you think the light shining on the billboard is bright enough?" Dad asked Jack.

Jack looked up at the sign again before he answered the question.

Suddenly, the large billboard tilted forward towards them.

It was going to land on them!

Just like the mining train cart monster, Jack used his arms to protect his head from the falling sign.

But nothing ever landed on him.

The billboard stopped just in time. Jack opened his eyes and looked up.

Mr. Bailey walked around to the back of the sign and pointed.

"See," he said. "We have thick chains mounted to the back of the billboard to stop it from actually falling on people."

Jack smiled. He was tricked again. But he was getting used to it. And started to actually like it.

Jack now really started to understand the concept of the haunted farm.

They continued on and walked by a campfire with a witch, and then crossed the newly constructed bridge, where there was someone in a troll costume hiding under it.

The troll didn't jump out at them though, but Mr. Bailey did stop and talk to him quickly before they hiked up the small hill towards the 3D maze.

Outside of the maze was a young teenage girl in a Little Red Riding Hood costume.

She was carrying a basket in her hand.

As Jack and Mr. Bailey arrived, she reached into her basket and pulled out two sets of cardboard glasses.

Mr. Bailey grabbed them both from her, and handed one pair to Jack.

"Here," Dad said. "Put these on."

Jack put on his 3D glasses.

"Have fun!" Little Red said.

"Thanks!" Jack replied.

They walked into the 3D maze slowly.

The music was louder in the maze, just like in the temple maze.

Jack also noticed something else. The lighting was different.

He noticed that the lights had a purple glow to them. Jack had seen those before. He sees them every year during the month of October.

"Are those blacklights?" Jack asked.

"You bet," Dad said. "They're perfect for keeping the 3D maze dark, but making all of the colors look bright."

"Why do these 3D glasses look different?" Jack said. "Don't they usually have one red lens and one blue lens?"

"That's right, they usually do. But these are a different type of 3D glasses," Dad said. "The different colored lenses allow your eyes to see the same image in two different ways, so it makes it appear to be 3D."

"Then what kind of 3D glasses are these?" Jack questioned.

"These glasses are based off of the colors you are looking at. When you paint colors of the rainbow onto a black surface, red looks like it's closest to you, and the blue colors look far away."

"What about the other colors?" Jack said.

"The rest of the rainbow colors fall in between. Orange, yellow, green are in the middle, just like a rainbow. It's called ChromaDepth."

Jack was admiring the 3D images all around him.

"So that's why the walls are all black, and everything is painted red, blue and yellow," Jack responded.

"Yup," Dad said.

The walls of each room in the 3D maze were all different.

Some rooms had clowns painted on the walls. Jack's favorite was the polka dot room.

"Cool!" Jack said. "It looks like I'm walking through a room of colorful stars floating in front of me."

"Notice how the red dots look closer to you than the blue dots?" Dad asked.

"Yes! And also how the yellow dots are in the middle, just like you said."

They walked around the 3D maze, and Jack realized, it wasn't really a maze. It was more of a guided path, just like the temple maze. It was still amazing.

Jack slowed down as they reached the next room. The walls were completely covered in colorful hockey masks.

They were surrounded by dozens of masks on each wall.

That's when Jack noticed one of the walls moved and someone was wearing one of the masks.

It looked like a mask came off of the wall and walked right towards him.

Jack thought that was a neat trick and should scare a lot of guests when they walked through.

"They are wearing black outfits, so they match the wall background, so all you can see is the mask. Cool, huh?" Dad said.

"This is my favorite so far," Jack said.

"3D mazes are very popular at Haunts," Dad said. "It's not as scary as the other parts, but it's really neat to walk through."

THE CORN MAZE

Jack and his Dad exited the back of the 3D maze and dropped their glasses into a collection basket.

"One more stop before we get to the corn maze," Dad said as they kept walking.

"Another maze?" Jack asked. "Is it like the temple maze and the 3D maze, or is it like a real maze?"

"The corn maze is an *actual* maze," Dad said. "You can truly get lost in it, especially since there are no lights in the cornfield."

"Besides the moonlight," Jack said.

"But we have many people in costume all around the inside of the corn maze, in case people get truly lost, they will scare them in the right direction," Dad explained.

Jack saw the next stop on the way to the corn maze.

Upside-down hanging Christmas trees.

"What's with the upside-down trees?" Jack said.

"We think this one will be a popular one too," Dad said. "To get to the corn maze, you need to push the swinging trees aside, and get by the scary monsters that lurk behind some of the trees."

Mr. Bailey paused.

"Want to go first?" Dad asked Jack.

Jack shook his head no. He wanted his Dad to walk through the trees first.

Mr. Bailey talked loudly to let the workers know that he and Jack were walking through the swinging trees, so they wouldn't jump out and scare them.

They were on a tight timeline, as the line at the temple was growing long with guests ready to enter the haunted farm.

Jack and his Dad came to the entrance of the corn maze. The corn looked really tall, so nobody would be able to see which way the corn maze paths went.

"I know the way through the maze, so follow me," Dad said.

It was completely dark outside, so Mr. Bailey took a flashlight out of his pocket and shined it onto the ground so they could see where they were going.

"Just watch out for monsters coming to scare you from behind," Dad said with a smirk.

"What kind of monsters?" Jack asked.

"We have all different kinds of monsters set up in the cornfield. We have some alien costumes, scarecrows, and some people are wearing ghillie suits," Dad said.

"What's a ghillie suit?" Jack said.

"Those are suits that make you look like a bush or a shrub. So they blend in with the area surrounding them. It's usually some kind of netting with leaves and branches on it."

Jack saw some of the corn stalks moving. He couldn't tell if it was from the cool breeze in the air, or if someone was hiding in the corn.

Jack really liked corn mazes during the daytime. The Bailey Family would visit several corn mazes every Autumn.

Many of the local farms had them. Small mazes, large mazes, didn't matter – Jack liked all of them.

They've done corn mazes before at nighttime, but not a *haunted* corn maze.

Jack noticed two things. First, the cornfield did not have lighting. Second, there was no music playing.

That made it even creepier.

As if walking around a cornfield at night wasn't spooky enough, they had to worry about people in costumes jumping out at them.

Jack walked through the rest of the maze carefully behind his Dad.

Every time Jack heard a new sound, he whipped his head around to make sure nobody was jumping out at him.

He heard all kinds of sounds.

Crackling of corn as they stepped on fallen or broken stalks, ears of corn that fell as they brushed up against them when they walked by, and even the occasional owl hooting in the distance.

Jack also thought about the corn snakes that could be slithering around, even though they were harmless.

Jack saw Mr. Bailey waving his flashlight as they walked through the remainder of the maze.

"What are you doing?" Jack asked.

"Trying to wipe out any real spider webs so I don't walk into one," Dad said. " I'm not a fan of walking my face into a real giant juicy spider web."

Jack got chills when he said that. It was

one thing to have that giant fake spider land on him in Phobia Forest, it was another thing to walk through a *real* spider web in the middle of the cornfield.

Especially the kinds of spiders that one would see on a farm in North Carolina.

"Once guests start walking through the farm and the corn, there won't be any webs," Dad said. "But the morning after, I bet there will be some new ones to clear out."

"Gross," Jack said. "I don't think I'll ever get used to the spiders and snakes in Charlotte."

"You and me both, Bud."

Jack observed that some parts of the corn maze were very narrow, and others had much wider paths.

"Hey Dad, why are all the paths different sizes?" Jack asked. "Is that to trick the people that walk through?"

"Good question, but that's not the reason," Dad said. "That's actually a clue, as to which way is the best way to go. You see, the more people that walk through the maze and complete it, the more that path and the corn will wear out."

"Wear out?" Jack said.

"Yes. Just like a pair of shoes. The more you use them, the treads wear out," Dad explained. "The same is true for the maze. The more people that walk through, the wider and well-traveled the path will get, making it easier to see which way to go."

"So the narrow paths are the wrong direction?" Jack asked.

"Not always, but usually."

Jack and his Dad got to the exit of the maze, and they found themselves in the parking lot.

"Hey, we did one big loop around the farm," Jack said.

"That's right Bud," Dad said. "Guests walk around the entire farm, then end at their car in the parking lot."

"So now what?" Jack said.

"Now the fun begins," Dad said. He put the walkie-talkie radio up to his mouth. "Team, we are officially ready to open Forbidden Farm! Let the first group through!"

THE AFTERMATH

The opening night for Forbidden Farm was a huge success.

Jack helped his Dad the entire night and loved the whole experience.

He loved being behind the scenes while he watched hundreds of people getting scared as they walked through all of the haunted attractions.

Jack was quite a help too.

He helped his Dad bring supplies like water bottles and radio batteries to many of the employees on the trail.

At the end of the night, when all of the guests had left the parking lot, it was time for Jack and his Dad to head home.

It was late, and way past Jack's bedtime.

Jack knew that his brother and sister would be sleeping, so he'd have to be quiet when he went upstairs to bed, so he wouldn't wake them up.

On the car ride home, Jack kept thinking about the entire experience.

The construction from earlier that Summer, the trip to Morris Costumes, the orientation and hotdogs roast, and the walk through before they opened – all great memories.

Mr. Bailey kept looking in the rearview mirror on the drive home, to watch his son Jack think about the evening.

"What's on your mind, Bud? Dad asked. "Are you going to be able to fall asleep tonight?"

"Yeah," Jack said.

"Are you going to have nightmares?"

"No, I'm fine. I understand it was all pretend. I think it helped being behind the scenes and watching how everything worked. It was awesome."

"I'm glad you liked it. And thanks for helping me out tonight, you were a big help," Dad said.

"Can I go back with you tomorrow night?" Jack asked.

Mr. Bailey laughed out loud.

"I don't think so, Bud. I don't want you to be exhausted for school on Monday. Coming home late on Friday and Saturday would make you really tired for next week."

Jack sighed. He really wanted to go back.

"Maybe we can go back during the day so I can show Olivia and Caleb everything that we did," Jack said.

"Maybe," Dad said. "Remember, they'll be sleeping when we get home, so we'll have to be extra quiet when we sneak into our beds."

"I know. I'll be silent."

A few minutes later, they arrived at home, and as promised, Jack quietly made his way upstairs.

He brushed his teeth and put his jammies on, and snuck into bed.

Jack had a hard time falling asleep.

Not because he was scared, but because he was excited. He couldn't stop thinking about all of the neat things he saw on the trail.

The temple, the mining train cart, the cemetery, phobia forest, the falling billboard, the troll and 3D maze, the swinging Christmas trees and the corn maze – everything was great.

He couldn't wait to tell his siblings and Mom about his evening.

Eventually, Jack fell asleep.

He didn't know what time he fell asleep, but it was much later than when he got into bed.

The next morning, the sun was barely up in the sky, and Jack was already awake.

He was up before everybody else in the house. He was going to burst if he didn't talk to anyone soon.

Jack and Caleb shared a bedroom, so Jack just sat in front of Wub's bed, waiting for him to open his eyes.

Wub was a late sleeper, so Jack knew it was going to be a while before he woke up, unless Jack started making loud sounds to make Caleb stir in bed.

Jack went across the hall, and peeked in on his parents' bedroom.

They were both sound asleep too.

Jack did what he thought would be the next best idea, and that was to wake up his sister Olivia.

Olivia's eyes were closed when Jack snuck into her room. He knew Olivia was a light sleeper though, unlike Wub.

Olivia had a sound machine that she listened to at night, to help her sleep. It played classical music.

Jack pushed the button on her machine to turn the music off.

Olivia immediately opened her eyes wide.

"Jack, what the heck?!" she bellowed.

Jack didn't know how to respond to that. He knew that he didn't want to wake up his parents or Wub, because he'd get in serious trouble.

"I thought you were already awake," Jack said.

"What made you think that, because my

bedroom door and eyes were closed?" Olivia said.

"I'm sorry, I couldn't wait to tell you about the farm last night!"

Olivia understood his excitement.

It's only been a few months since Olivia and her Dad went through her first haunted attraction, the Mysterious Mansion, during Spring Break.

She slowly sat up to listen.

Jack told her about the entire evening, and Olivia was genuinely interested in his story.

She asked lots of questions about the Forbidden Farm, because she was curious to learn the difference between an outdoor haunted attraction, like the farm Jack walked through, and the indoor haunt that her and Mr. Bailey went through earlier that year.

After Jack told his story and Olivia finished asking questions, Jack got to the real reason why he woke Olivia up.

"Do you remember on the way home from Tennessee earlier this year, you said you were going to start a scary afterschool club?" Jack asked.

"Of course I remember," Olivia said.

"Whatever happened to that?" Jack said.

"I didn't have enough time to start the club before Summer Break."

"What if we started the afterschool club this year?" Jack whispered.

"Does that mean you're interested in the club?" Olivia said eagerly.

117

"After going through my first haunted attraction, I can see how that club could be fun."

"We can't just start a club, we'd have to get approval from our principal," Olivia said.

"How would the club work?" Jack asked.

"Well, you know how there are other afterschool specials? Like the inventors club, the tennis and lacrosse clubs, the Lego club, and all the others?" Olivia said.

Jack knew what she was talking about, he'd been in several of those clubs already.

"Well, we'd have a club where kids would get together after school and tell ghost stories," Olivia continued.

"It would need to have a cool name to

get other kids excited," Jack answered.

"I already have an idea for the name of the afterschool club," Olivia said.

Jack awaited her response.

"The Cobweb Kids Club."

ABOUT THE AUTHOR

John C. Abrahamson was born and raised in New England, before moving to North Carolina to raise his family. John has many passions. Besides writing, he enjoys traveling, hiking, reading, disc golf, jet skiing, and most importantly, spending time with his family.

AUTHOR'S NOTE

Thank you all for taking the time to read The Cobweb Kids. This second installment of the series is half of a true story.

Halloween has always been a special time for me, growing up in New England, Autumn and Halloween were very special.

Vibrant foliage. Trick-or-treating for hours as a kid, filling up pillowcases of candy. And making scary movies with my friends was always fun.

I even remember making a haunted house in my friends grandmother's basement when we were really young.

I continued that as an adult.

The part of this story that is true, is that I actually did start a haunted attraction in

Mooresville, NC – called Forbidden Farm.

Many of the scares in this story were also true, which is how I have all of those pictures in each chapter.

The part that isn't true, is that Jack walked through with me. He was only one month old back then, not a third grader like he is now.

The cool thing is, almost a decade later, the farm is still sponsoring the haunted attraction.

I believe the temple is still there, and everything.

My intent for this second book, and the series of books that will follow, is to introduce a younger audience to spooky content.

A younger version of Goosebumps, if

you will.

If you like the Cobweb series, please continue to follow Olivia, Jack and Caleb as they begin their Cobweb Kids Club at school, and experience new adventures.

Follow me on social media with the information on the next page, or simply check back with my website for upcoming project announcements and public appearances.

Thank you so much, I appreciate you all!

#WriteOn

Connect with John on social media to follow his current and upcoming projects.

Twitter: @JohnTheNovelist

Facebook Page: JohnTheNovelist

Author Website: JohnAbrahamson.com

Made in the USA
Middletown, DE
04 October 2016